Angela and Bear

Holt, Rinehart and Winston · New York

Angela and Bear

by Susan Jeschke

Library of Congress Cataloging in Publication Data

Jeschke, Susan.
  Angela and Bear.

  SUMMARY: With the help of her magic crayons,
Angela acquires what she wants most — a real bear.
  [1. Magic — Fiction. 2. Bears — Fiction.]
I. Title.   PZ7.J553An   [E]   78-15224
ISBN 0-03-044511-6

For two of the finest,
Roger Jeschke,
and my sister, Jane Kochman

"You promised to play with me," Angela said.
"When I'm through reading the newspaper. Here, why don't
you go to the zoo?" her father said, handing her a quarter.

Just inside the zoo was an old man selling things.
Angela looked everything over and decided to buy a box of crayons.
"A good choice," the man said. "Those are magic crayons.
They make magic pictures," he added.

Angela slipped the crayons
into her purse and went to see
Lola, her favorite bear.
Lola's keeper came by and waved
to Angela.
"Hello, Lola Polah," Angela said.
Lola smiled back.
Angela spent the afternoon with Lola.
"Goodbye, Lola," she said
when it was time to leave.
"See you tomorrow.
Remember, I love you."

"If only I had a bear of my own," Angela thought.
But every time she asked for one her father would say, "No, you can't always have something just because you want it."
"Anyway, today I have magic crayons," she said.
At home, she took out her crayons and began to draw a bear.

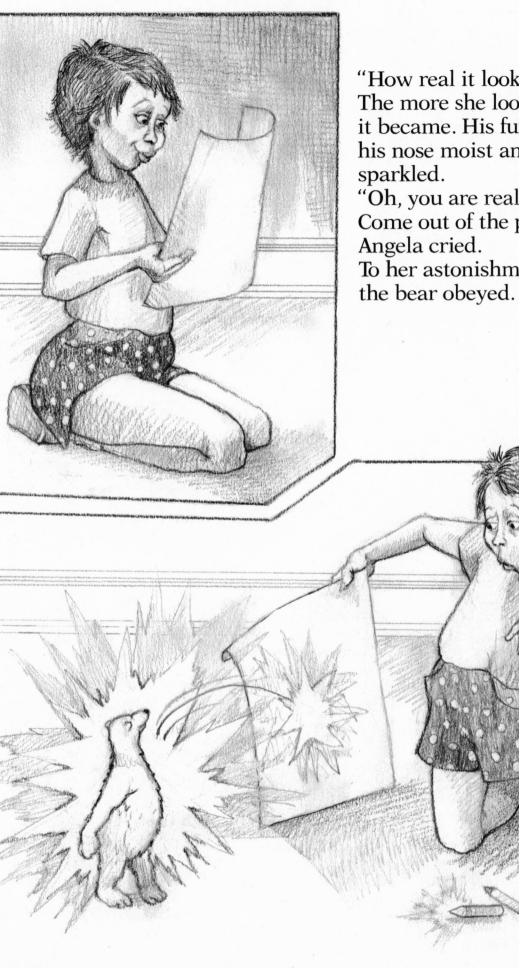

"How real it looks!" she said.
The more she looked the more real
it became. His fur looked furry,
his nose moist and his eyes
sparkled.
"Oh, you are real! Come out!
Come out of the picture!"
Angela cried.
To her astonishment,
the bear obeyed.

Once out, he grew until he was a full-sized bear.
"My bear! My very own bear!" Angela cried.

Angela couldn't sleep that night.
The next morning she got ready
for school.
"How can I hide you?" Angela asked.
Bear nodded to the picture.
"Good idea!" Angela said.
"Then I can take you with me
wherever I go."
Bear shrank until he was small
enough to get back in.

Wherever Angela went she took the picture.
She always looked for secret places before commanding Bear
to come out of the picture. Bear always obeyed.
Sometimes they were discovered.
"A bear!" some frightened person would exclaim.
"Oh no, everyone thinks that. He is really a dog,"
Angela would say.
Then Bear would heel and bark.
Angela had trained him to do this in such emergencies.

Bear was always happiest
when they did new things.

There was no lack of things to keep Bear happy
throughout the summer…

…and the autumn.

But winter was the happiest season for Bear.

Sometimes he didn't want
to get back into the picture.
Angela would have to
tempt him back by drawing
fish in the picture.

With spring came the rain —
and staying indoors.
Angela did everything
she could to please him.
It wasn't until she found
a book with pictures of
bears that he began to smile.
This gave Angela an idea.
"We will visit Lola!" she said.
Angela got into her rainhat
and boots and Bear got into
his picture and they set out.

Victoria's Adventure
Susan Jeschke

Lola immediately recognized Angela.
Then Angela took out her picture.
Without waiting for Angela
to say, "Come out, Bear,"
Bear jumped out.
Bear and Lola gazed at each other.

Then they both let out a joyful growl and dove into the pool.

"OK, that's enough, time to go home," Angela said.
But Bear shook his head NO.
"What?!—You must. You are mine, and you must obey me,"
Angela said.
She tried tempting him back in the usual way,
but Bear was having too good a time with Lola to leave.
Finally Angela gave up and ran home crying.
"It's just not fair, he's mine," she sobbed.

The next day her father read her an article from the newspaper,
about how a new bear had suddenly appeared at the zoo,
and nobody seemed to know where it had come from.
"I know all about it," Angela snapped. "He's mine!"
"Oh...I see...Well, I would like to have a look at 'your' bear.
How about you and I going to the zoo?" he said.

The cage was surrounded by people admiring the new bear.
"What do you think of our wonderful new bear?" the keeper said.
"Lola really has found a friend," he added.
"I must find a way to get him back," Angela thought.

Every day she went
to the zoo.
She pleaded, begged
and ordered, but Bear
would not leave Lola.
Finally Angela had an idea.
She took her magic crayons
and drew a picture
of the polar North —
snow, ice, even a few fish
lying in the snow.
The ice glittered and
a cold wind blew sharply
against her.
She waited for a very
warm night and set out
for the zoo,
taking a fish from the icebox,
a string, and the picture.

Lola and Bear were both asleep.
Angela tied the string around
the fish and threw it
into the cage.
It hit Bear smack on the nose.
He wakened and sleepily
followed the smell.

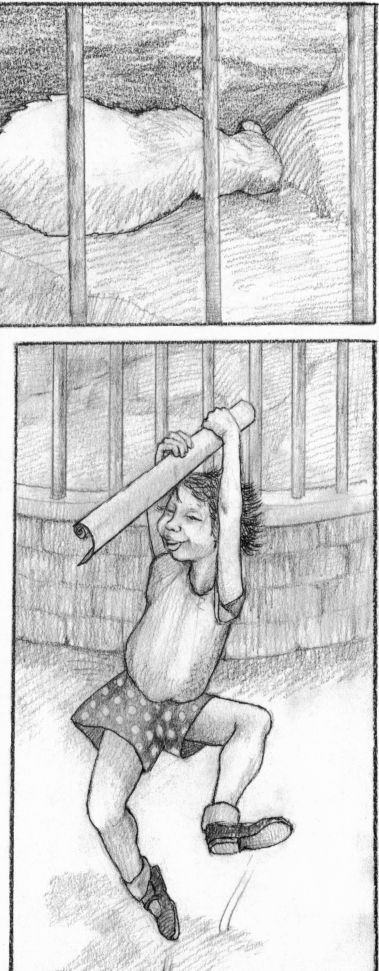

Angela pulled the fish
slowly towards the picture.
Just as Bear grabbed for it,
she yanked it under the picture.
Bear stared at the picture
as if hypnotized. Then he grew
smaller and smaller
until he disappeared into it.

Angela hurried home.
"Come out, Bear," she commanded. He did, but was dazed
and puzzled to find himself in Angela's room
and he fell off to sleep.
Angela lay awake thinking of all the good times
they would again have.

The next morning news of Bear's disappearance
from the zoo was on television.
"Everyone is going to die of a broken heart if this bear
isn't found," her father said.
Angela tried to comfort her father. "Well—everyone
can't have something just because they want it.
Anyway—they might find him," she said.

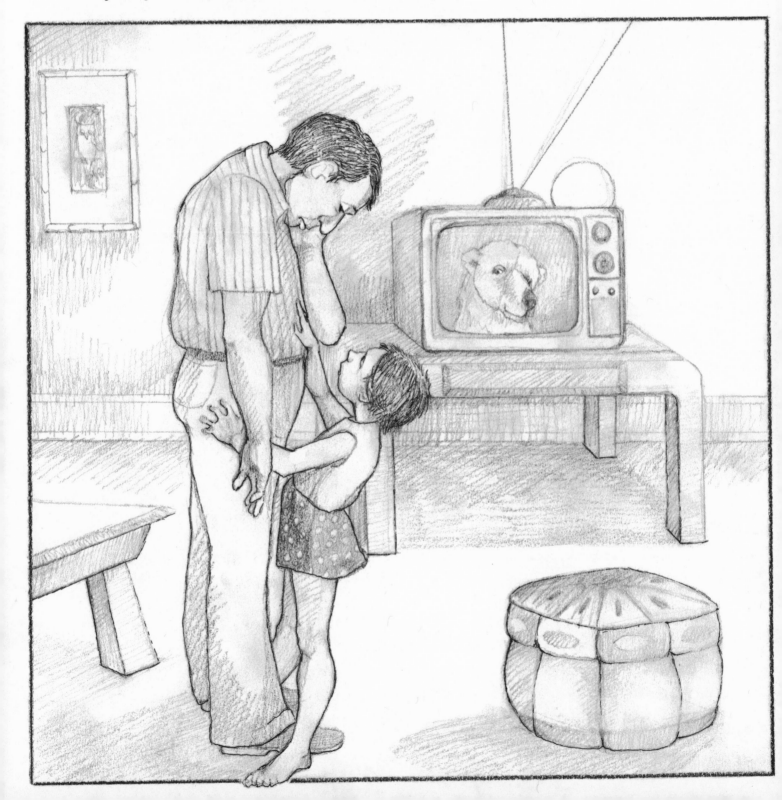

She returned to her room.
Bear was awake.
"We're going on a picnic.
I know how you love picnics,"
Angela said.
But Bear turned his back
on Angela and went back
into his picture.
"We can also go for a swim,"
she added.
Still Bear did not respond—
and this began to trouble Angela.

She packed the picture into the picnic basket and walked to the zoo. Her father was right. Everyone was unhappy. She overheard people saying, "Imagine, someone stealing our lovely bear." "What a terrible person!" "I hope the poor bear is all right—how empty the zoo is without him!"

The keeper was slumped
on a bench.
"I'm going to sit here
forever until that bear is back,"
he said.
Lola would not come
out of her cave.

Angela found a secret spot for the picnic.
"Come out, Bear," she said. But he wouldn't.
It was a very lonely picnic for Angela.
She ate only a few bites of an apple and watched Bear watching her.
Finally Angela couldn't stand Bear's sad face anymore.
"I like you best when you are happy!" she said,
and rolled up the picture.

She returned to the zoo.
Everyone had gone home but the keeper, who was asleep.
"Bear," she whispered to the picture,
"come out. I've brought you back to Lola."
Bear jumped out and hugged Angela.

Then he growled loudly.
The keeper awoke and led Bear back into the cage.

"Goodnight, goodnight and goodbye, Bear," Angela said.

She threw her picture in a trash basket, and ran home.